Five short tales about unusual children

Bailey Av Elliott - Middleton

www.emporiumorionis.com

2022

I dedicate this book to all Indigo Children, Crystal Children, Rainbow Children, high-sensitivity Empaths, and those who always stand up for children, animals, nature and Mother Earth.

Love our Mother Earth, love animals, trees and all nature, love each other and respect every life.

May love, peace, and light always be with you and in you.

Bless you.

Emporium Orionis and Orion Creations, 2022

Thank you

Thank you for choosing our book.
The book you hold in your hands is our first children's book
about extraordinary young individuals, and it brings good values
and lessons to other children who read these stories.

This book is also a reminder to be kind, to have a cheerful and
good heart and an open mind every day because we never
know what may happen.

I hope you enjoy a beautiful, peaceful lifestyle as much as we do.

You can use this book as an excellent excuse to spend more time
with your child and read it aloud to your child before falling
asleep. Enjoy your precious time together.
Bless you

Celine

Once upon a time, there was a little girl named Celine who had a big imagination - that was what her parents thought about her - and she also had a lovely and caring heart.

Celine was always kind to everyone she met. She loved all animals and nature and always helped take care of birds and trees, and flowers. She even fed stray cats and birds.

Celine wasn't afraid of spiders or disgusted by earthworms because she loved all animals equally. She always greeted her neighbours and teachers and said hi to all the kids and dogs on the street.

One day, she spotted a little robin on the ground. Its wing was broken. Celine quickly scooped the poor robin up, covered it with her handkerchief, and brought it home to take care of this little bird.

She made a soft bed out of a shoebox and some old cloth and found some food and water for the bird. She even named the bird Mr. Dursley.

Every day, Celine would visit Mr. Dursley to play with him a little and take care of him until, one day, he was well enough to fly away. Celine was so happy and proud as she watched Mr. Dursley soar away into the sky.

Celine continued to be kind and help animals, no matter how small the task. She helped pick up litter from the street and put it into rubbish bins.

She helped her parents plant trees, grow organic vegetables and fruits, and create a beautiful butterfly and bees garden filled with colourful flowers and plants.

With her grandpa's little help, she also built a wooden feeding house with a roof for birds. Mr. Dursley was a frequent

visitor of this beautiful house. He always brought all his family and other bird friends to Celine's garden.

All the birds sing beautiful songs every spring, summer and autumn while visiting Celine's garden like they will saying thank you for the food and care. Celine loved her bird friends and their songs. She really enjoyed feeding them and having little chats with them.

They have only been quiet during windy and snowy winter but visit Celine for delicious food every day during cold winter days.

Celine loved the idea of taking care of our planet in other ways too. She turned off lights at home when she left her room to save energy and put empty jars and baskets in the garden to catch rainwater for watering her indoor plants. She always sorted the garbage into the right boxes and recycled and used reusable bags when shopping with her parents.

Her parents and grandparent were very proud of her in every way because she was such a loving girl.

Celine's kindness and love of all people, nature and animals inspired everyone around her. She made everyone happy and smile and comfortable.

She is an excellent example of the kind heart and soul we all can be. Being friendly, polite and loving costs nothing, but it makes a significant difference for everyone we meet daily.

Be kind and brave to show other people, animals and trees your big loving heart because I strongly believe that you have a big, big heart and care about our home - our planter Earth and every living being that lives on Earth. The animals and nature: trees, grass, water, and air need our care and support. Let's take good care of them together, like loving Celine does.

Matt

Once upon a time, there was a young boy named Matt who had a very curious mind and an affinity for books. Matt was also extremely empathetic and understanding of the people around him, and he often felt the emotions of those around him as if they were his own.

Unfortunately, Matt often found himself an outcast among his peers who did not understand his sensitive nature. They would call him "weird" and often leave him out of conversations or activities, making him feel even more alone.

Though Matt often felt isolated and misunderstood, he found solace in books. He would escape into the pages of his favourite stories and explore the lives and adventures of the characters he read about.

Matt often lost himself in these stories and created his own magical world where he felt understood and connected to the characters he read about. He found comfort in their struggles and joy in their victories, and he often felt a sense of peace as he read.

But what is most important is that Matt started writing his own tales and put the dream worlds and adventures on pages he already held in his imagination.

The characters he created and made alive in his stories had special powers to make the worlds where they lived a better, unique and good place to live for all the creatures.

So those characters, the kids to be more precise, have, for example, the power of creation from nothing to something.

Believe me or not, they could literally make a real skyscraper in front of your eyes in one second just from the air.

The others have the ability to fly. Very high and very fast.

There were others with the power of being invisible. So, those kids could come in everywhere they wanted, listen to people's conversations, especially those bad ones, and use this knowledge to help the world. So, not every eavesdropping is a bad thing.

The others have the power to change solid matter structure into something else.

There were also kids with the power of healing.

And the power to make other creatures calm and lovable, especially those who were unkind and aggressive.

And the power of travelling between different dimensions without a problem.

And the power to grow unique plants in a demanding environment like, for example, a desert, so the desert would look like a beautiful wood with waterfalls in a millisecond and in this wood, they would create many different species, exotic fruits and maybe castles, Fun lands and Luna Parks with rollercoasters. Really, whatever they liked, they could magically make it come true.

Matt's imagination created more special kids with superpowers whenever he needed someone to do something good for the world.

He created an army of unique kids with superpowers. The kids were like Matt, good-hearted, smart and wanted to do good for others and the world.

No matter how big this world could be or how many of them they could visit.

From this love of books and writing, Matt developed a better understanding of the people around him and learned how to express his emotions more clearly. He also became more confident and found the courage to make friends and be part of the group.

And day by day, in the real world, Matt started seeing more and more of such good, unique kids. They may not have such vivid superpowers, but they were brave enough and good enough to come and say hi to Matt, make friends with him, be kind to one another and other kids, and be polite to adults as well.

And in those small things, in those good hearts and intentions, magic can appear silently and unnoticed. It may do the magic trick and empower these children with extraordinary abilities for the good of us all and the good of all worlds.

Be good, be kind and maybe, just maybe, one day, magic can find you and make you a superpower kid too.

You never know. Believe in magic. Believe in good. Never stop believing. And remember we are all different, with different experience, believes, thoughts and dreams.

Learn to accept differences more, keep your mind and heart open, and never make assumptions, criticise or judge.

Instead, connect with others, be patient with them, be more understanding and accepting, care more and focus on good things only.

And one more thing, remember if other children are not positive and friendly to you, if they misbehave and do wrong things you don't have to make friends with them, you don't have to follow them or listen.

You can only choose to be friends with those who match your nature and are polite and friendly to you. Who you want to play with is always your choice, and no one has the right to make you like them and accept their mean behaviour.

Lyla

Once upon a time, there was a little girl named Lyla who was very different from the other kids who lived in her neighbourhood.

She had this unique ability that no one else seemed to have: she could talk to animals and make them understand her perfectly, even though they spoke different languages.

It wasn't something she had to think about; it just came naturally to her. Whenever she was near animals, she felt a special connection between them and herself, and she could understand what they were saying.

Lyla was a shy and timid girl, and she lived with her parents in a big house away from the town and other children, so she didn't have many friends her age.

But talking to animals wasn't the only thing that was unique about Lyla. She also had an imaginary friend she loved playing with when her parents were busy working. His name was Elio, and he lived in a faraway land.

Whenever Lyla felt lonely, Elio would come to visit her and play together. He was always there for her when she needed someone to talk to, and she trusted him completely that she would tell him all her secrets, and he would listen intently without judging or criticising her.

That was why she always enjoyed his company, as he made her feel better and less alone.

Unfortunately, Lyla's parents didn't understand her and kept telling her that Elio wasn't real but only her imagination. They constantly tried to convince her to forget about him, but for Lyla, Elio was real.
He was her only friend, and she couldn't imagine not having him in her life.

One day, Lyla decided that she would prove to her parents that Elio was real. She went to her room, closed the door, and opened the portal to a different world, just like Elio had taught her.

She decided to find him in a faraway land and bring him home to introduce him to her parents.

In the different dimensions, she found very bizarre-looking but friendly creatures, and she talked to them and asked them to help her find a way to prove that Elio was real and, most of all, to help her find him.

The animals told her that if she believed in Elio, then she didn't have to worry about what other people say about him or judge her beliefs because her beliefs are her business, not theirs.

- But, I am a little girl - said Lyla - and I have to listen to what my parent say.
- But your parents might be wrong sometimes - said both creatures in unison
- They are right most of the time, but not always. You might be right, too, you know. And they might be wrong this time.
- The creatures looked at one another, they nodded and continued.

- Because you are still a little girl, it doesn't mean you don't know what is true and what isn't, or you don't know what you believe in, what you see or what is good for you and what is not.

You have to believe in yourself more and trust your feelings. We will help you to find Elio. I think we might know where he is. We will make this journey flying through the sky land.

- Jump on my back - said one of them in one voice - and make yourself comfortable.

They flew above the clouds and gigantic tree crowns, and Lyla could see big cities in those green crowns, much different than those she knew on Earth.

She was mesmerised by its lights and splendour. She never saw so many tremendous sculptures and monuments.

Suddenly, she heard Celtic music playing in the distance. And then, when the clouds passed away, and the sun came out, she saw him sitting on a hill.

She felt so relieved because they had found him. It was Elio playing the Theremin, not even touching the instrument, but beautiful music echoed around.

Elio was very surprised when he saw her, but a big smile grew on his face at the same time.
- This time, it is you who came to visit me - Elio said and hugged Lyla - To what do I owe this visit? - Elio asked.
- I want you to meet my parents - said Lyla.
- No way, they would not understand. They would not believe you anyway - said Elio - I don't want to meet your parents.

I don't want them to meet me. You are my friend, and I only want you to see me and be my friend, not them - cried Elio.

- Can't we just go and have some fun? I will show you something you will love! I'm sure about it! – said Elio.

And Lyla gave up the idea of introducing Elio to her parents. Maybe he is right. Perhaps they would not understand even if they had him in front of their eyes.

- Let's have fun, then - she said - show me what you promised! I'm so excited! - she cried.

And Elio took her hand. They thanked the creatures that helped bring Lyla here and ran down the hill straight to the ocean, where they met a family of whales.

Both Elio and Lyla could talk to the whales, and the whales felt so thrilled talking to the human being that they decided to take the kids on an underwater adventure.

Lyla spent the whole day playing with Elio and the whales in the ocean. She felt so happy and delighted, but at the end of the day, she had to get back home because her parent would soon be finishing their work and they might realise that she was not at home.

Come on, show me how you open the portal - said Elio, smiling.
Lyla focused and opened the portal in front of them. Elio was so proud of her and could not believe she could do it with such grace and lightness.

- You learned well, Lyla. You can visit me now anytime you want. You don't have to wait for me to come to see you anymore.
- said Elio.
- Yes, and I will. There are so many exciting things you can show me in your world - said Lyla and hugged Elio goodbye.

Lyla got back to her room. She could not stop smiling. And then she decided that she would keep Elio and his world secret and never mention them to her parents again. If they chose to not believe her, then so be it.
They don't need to know everything about her.
- I would let them think Elio was just my imagination - decided Lyla, and she left her room to see her parents downstairs in the kitchen.

Ben

Once upon a time, there was a boy named
Ben. He was a beautiful and brilliant soul.

Most of his time, he lived in his own
world, created in his head, where
everything had its particular place, and
everything happened in the right order.

Ben was an autistic boy but being autistic
didn't define him as a person but gave
him this unique ability to see numbers in

colours and solve very complex math problems without using a calculator or computer. Which surprised many adults and made him, in their eyes, super bright.

How he saw the world around him was slightly different from other children. He often felt like he was on the outside looking in and had difficulty connecting with people around him.

He didn't like mixing the colours of the food on his plate or in his daily clothes. But he was very well-organised and precise in everything he was doing.

Ben loved mathematics, physics, and astronomy, but most of all, he loved everything about Christmas.

He loved Christmas time, ornaments, decorations, cards, garlands, colourful lights and presents wrapped in Christmas paper and shiny paper bags.

It was very close to Christmas this year, and Ben could not wait until they started decorating their home and buying and decorating a real Christmas tree.

One day, about ten days before Christmas, Ben was sitting in his room, feeling more alone than usual. He was never desperate for someone, but he needed to feel some kind of connection in his unique way.

He had an ants farm in his room in a glassy aquarium. That was the only pet his mum could agree to as she was allergic to almost everything and couldn't stand any pet at home. But what kind of connection can you make with ants?

He didn't have many friends and usually spent his days alone. Although his parents hired a lady who took care of him, making him meals and checking if he was doing okay, he didn't like her in his room or to be interrupted, so she usually spent her working hours downstairs in the living room watching telly.

Ben was thinking about the upcoming Christmas, how big the new Christmas tree will be, and what kind of present he would like to get this year when something strange and unexpected happened. He heard a whisper coming from his closed.

It was a voice he had never heard before, yet it sounded so familiar.

The voice said, "Hi, Ben. Remember me? I am an angel sent from heaven to look after you and keep you company whenever you need me."

Ben was surprised. He had no idea how to respond. But he was comforted somehow by the thought that someone was looking out for him, but on the other hand, he never believed in angels, and how on earth an angel ended up in his closet?

So Ben said nothing, just sat still and waited, observing the closet door.
- Can I come out of the closet? - asked the angel - There's not much room here, and it's dark, and I think I can see a spider. I hate spiders.

- You can - said Ben, and said nothing more.

- Great, thanks, Ben - said the angel and entered the room, brushing the dust off his wings - You probably thinking, why am I here and whether I am real or just pretending to be an angel from heaven, right, Ben?

- Yes, and yes - said Ben looking at the angel with curiosity.

- It's nearly Christmas, and I wanted to do something good for human beings. This is what angels do, am I right, Ben? This is what angels do. So, I thought I would entertain you a bit before your favourite time of the year and spend some time accompanying you. I hate seeing people sad. So, what do you say, Ben? Can I visit you and have a little chat with you before Christmas?

- Yes, and yes - said Ben again, as he didn't like not being polite, and he always wanted to answer all the questions others asked him.
- Brilliant! - said angel with enthusiasm. - What would you like to do first, Ben? or maybe you would like to talk about something with me?
- I would like to go camping with my parents to the Forrest of Dean this Christmas - responded Ben without hesitation, and he actually felt surprised as he didn't think about this before.
- Oh, camping - angel thought - Have you ever been to Forrest of Dean for camping, Ben?
- I haven't - Ben said.
- I can whisper to your parent's ears this and that if you like - angel said.
- Okay - said Ben and smiled.

That was the first smile in a long time and made Ben feel good and positive. When Ben was wandering in his mind thinking about what Angel said, the door opened, and Ben's father entered his room.

- What you up to, Ben? - father asked - I just spoke with your mother, and we thought maybe we could go camping to Forest of Dean for Christmas this year. What do you think, Ben? - father looked into Ben's eyes.

Would you like to spend Christmas at a camp? We, of course, will take all your presents with us, for you to open them on Christmas Day, and all your favourite meals, warm clothes, and whatever you like. We will have an open fire and play in the snow. Huh, Ben, do you like the idea?

- Okay. Yes, and yes - said Ben, and patted his father on the shoulder as he used to do instead of hugging people because he never felt comfortable hugging others.
- Well, then, start packing as we are leaving soon. Your mother already booked camping for us, because she knew somehow you would love to go. Isn't she a brilliant mind-reader, Ben? She knows everything.

Ben felt delighted. This was precisely what he wanted to do this Christmas, but how his father knew that? Was that the angel to whisper into his father's and mother's ears this and that like he said he will?
And where was the angel? Where did he go? Will Ben see him again?

Ben thought about the angel for a while and started packing his winter clothes and favourite books into his backpack.

So, Ben went camping with his parents this Christmas. They played in the snow for hours, barbequing and roasting sausages on the fire, telling stories and having a wonderful time together. Finally, he could spend his favourite time of the year with his parents and have all their attention on him.

From then on, the angel visited Ben every day. He never disappeared forever. He just made some space for Ben to enjoy precious time with his parents, which never happens very often.

Ben and angel talked and laughed together when Ben needed company, and Ben finally felt a connection with someone. He felt like he had a friend.

The angel also comforted Ben when his parents were too busy working on their computers and on calls and gave him the needed attention. The angel reminded him that he was loved by his parents in their way and that he was never alone.

Ben loved having his angel friend around. He admired his enormous wings and the light beams shining from his heart centre and above his head.

Ben and his angel remained close friends for years to come. Ben would often talk to the angel when he was feeling down, and the angel was always there to offer advice and comfort.

Ben's autism diagnosis did not stop him from living a happy and fulfilling life. He could find joy in the small things and connect with others in meaningful ways. He had found a true friend in his angel, but he became more open to other people and decided to apply for a physics and astronomy course for special children, which made his parents very happy and proud.

Ben's story reminds us that we all need love and support, even those who may feel on the outside looking in. With a bit of help from others, Ben could find true happiness and open up for new adventures in his life with enthusiasm and willingness.

Jack

Once upon a time, a boy named Jack lived in a small village by the sea. He spent most of his days playing on the beach and chasing seagulls.

One day, while walking near the beach, Jack noticed a white and ginger kitten looking at him with gentle eyes. He had never seen such a beautiful kitten in his entire life, so he approached him and petted him.

The boy wondered if the kitten had lost its mother or if someone had abandoned him alone. He knew people in the village, but he hadn't heard of any of them having a mother cat with kittens this season, so he assumed that maybe someone else in the neighbouring village had abandoned a kitten, so Jack decided to take care of him.

The boy's mother loved all animals, and Jack knew that she would be happy to take the kitten home and let the boy keep him.

The kitten wasn't afraid at all and allowed the boy to pet him, and the two quickly became best friends.

Jack and the kitten would spend their days together, playing in the sand and exploring the village. But their favourite thing to do was to go on imaginary journeys. The boy would tell the kitten about places he had only ever dreamed of visiting, and the kitten's eyes would light up with excitement.

On one of these imaginary journeys, the boy and the kitten sailed to a beautiful island full of exotic animals and plants. They explored the island and made friends with the animals, and the kitten even found a perfect spot where they could take a nap in the sun.

Jack and the kitten went on many more amazing journeys together, and their friendship was solid and lasting. No matter what happened, the boy knew that his cat friend would always be there for him.

The kitten grew quickly into a strong and intelligent tomcat and began showing extraordinary abilities. The tomcat could communicate now with Jack mentally without using words, and Jack could hear his voice in his head, and he didn't have to use words either to answer the cat.

One day during their lazy day at the beach, tomcat said to Jack - Hey, Jack, wanna see something that I just discovered?
- Yes, sure. What is that, my friend? - Jack replied.
- Okay, so close your eyes, relax and let me take you somewhere - Said tomcat.

- Wait! What? Where? - Jack jumped to his feet.
- Oh, relax, Jack, don't you trust me? That will be such good fun. I promise!

And tomcat took Jack on a journey into different galaxies and solar systems. They saw the stars were born, they admired stunning views and colours, and when Jack and tomcat were returning, they flew through Orion's Belt in the constellation of Orion.

The tomcat showed Jack Orion's seven major stars. At the centre of four stars that outline the giant rectangular shape Rigel, Betelgeuse, Bellatrix, and Saiph lie three stars of Orion's Belt - Alnitak, Alnilam and Mintaka.

Jack loved Orion and loved the galaxy journey with his best friend.

Before Jack met his tomcat and rescued him from being a stray cat, his life was a bit boring, but now he has gained a best friend.

They always do something interesting and exciting together, and now they can even travel through the universe and talk to each other without saying a word out loud.

- What an exciting life! - said Jack - Thank Gods I took you from the street and made you my best friend. Life with you is so much better than my life before you. Please stay with me forever!

But tomcat only smiled and said nothing to Jack.

Tomcat knew that his time was limited and much shorter than human life, so he wanted to enjoy every moment without wasting a thing, and Jack was the best company the tomcat could ever wish for in this life.

Jack found out what tomcat was thinking about and said - I know that cats live not that long like we do, and I promise that I will take good care of you, feed you well and love you forever because you are my best friend.

I will never, ever let you down, and I will never let anyone hurt you. Let's get back home my dearest friend. Mum must have already prepared something delicious for us for dinner. I'm hungry!
- Me, too! - exclaimed the tomcat.

And the boy and the cat walked back along the forest path from the beach to the house, smiling happily that they had each other for life. That was all they needed.

...and dinner. Yes, they need a delicious Mummy's dinner now too.

Printed in Great Britain
by Amazon

33868647R00037